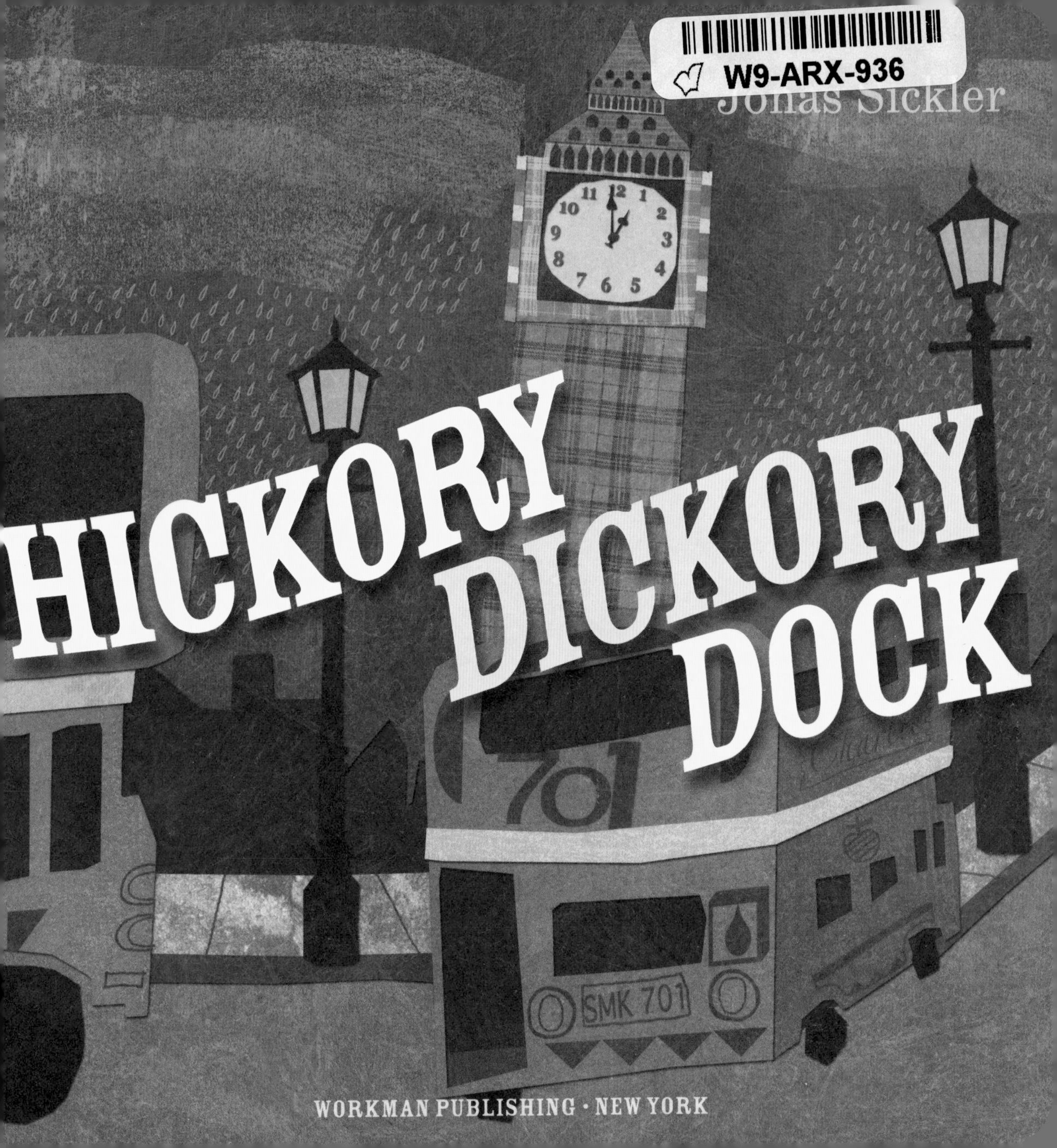
Jonas Sickler
HICKORY DICKORY DOCK
701
SMK 701
WORKMAN PUBLISHING · NEW YORK

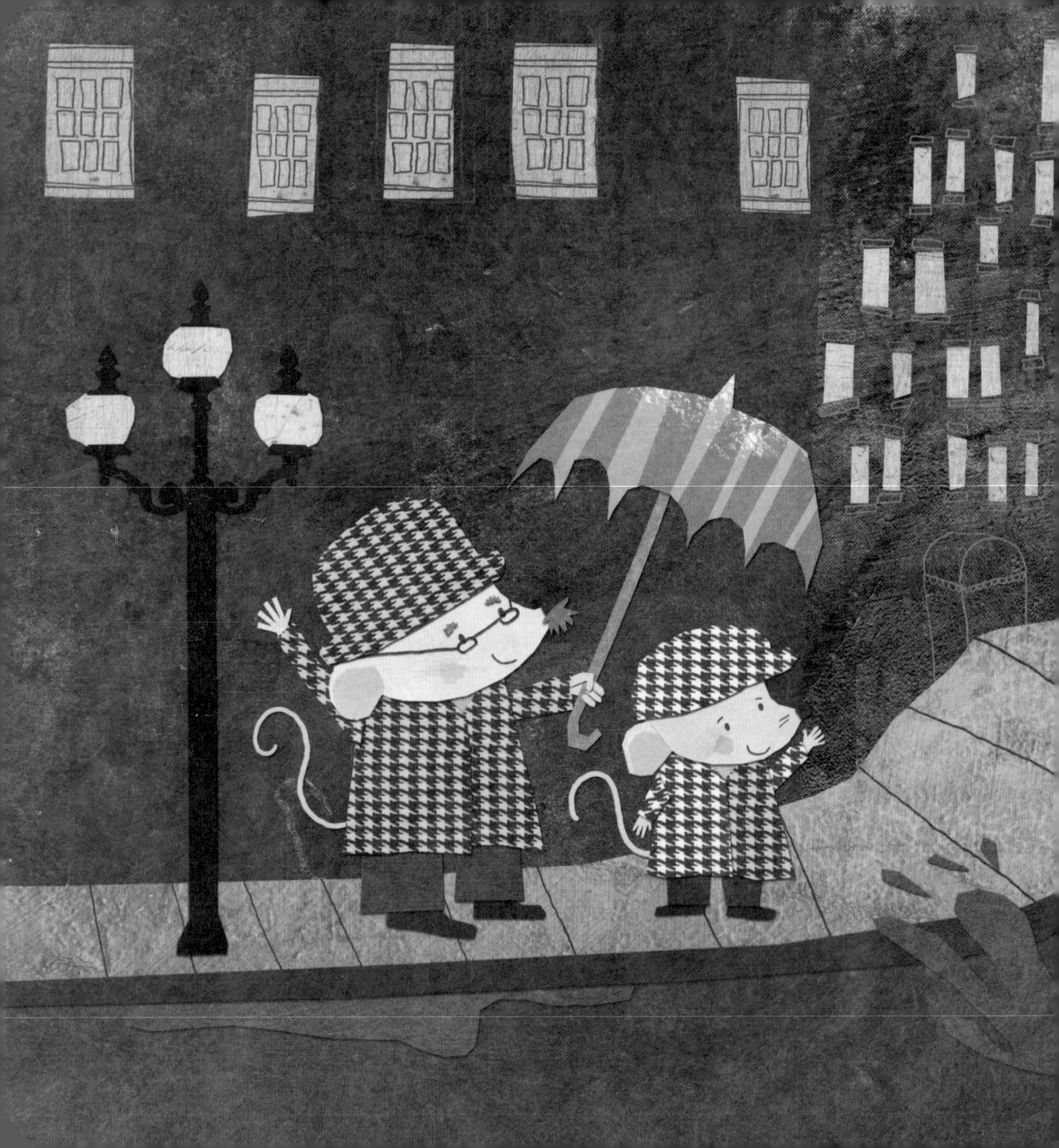

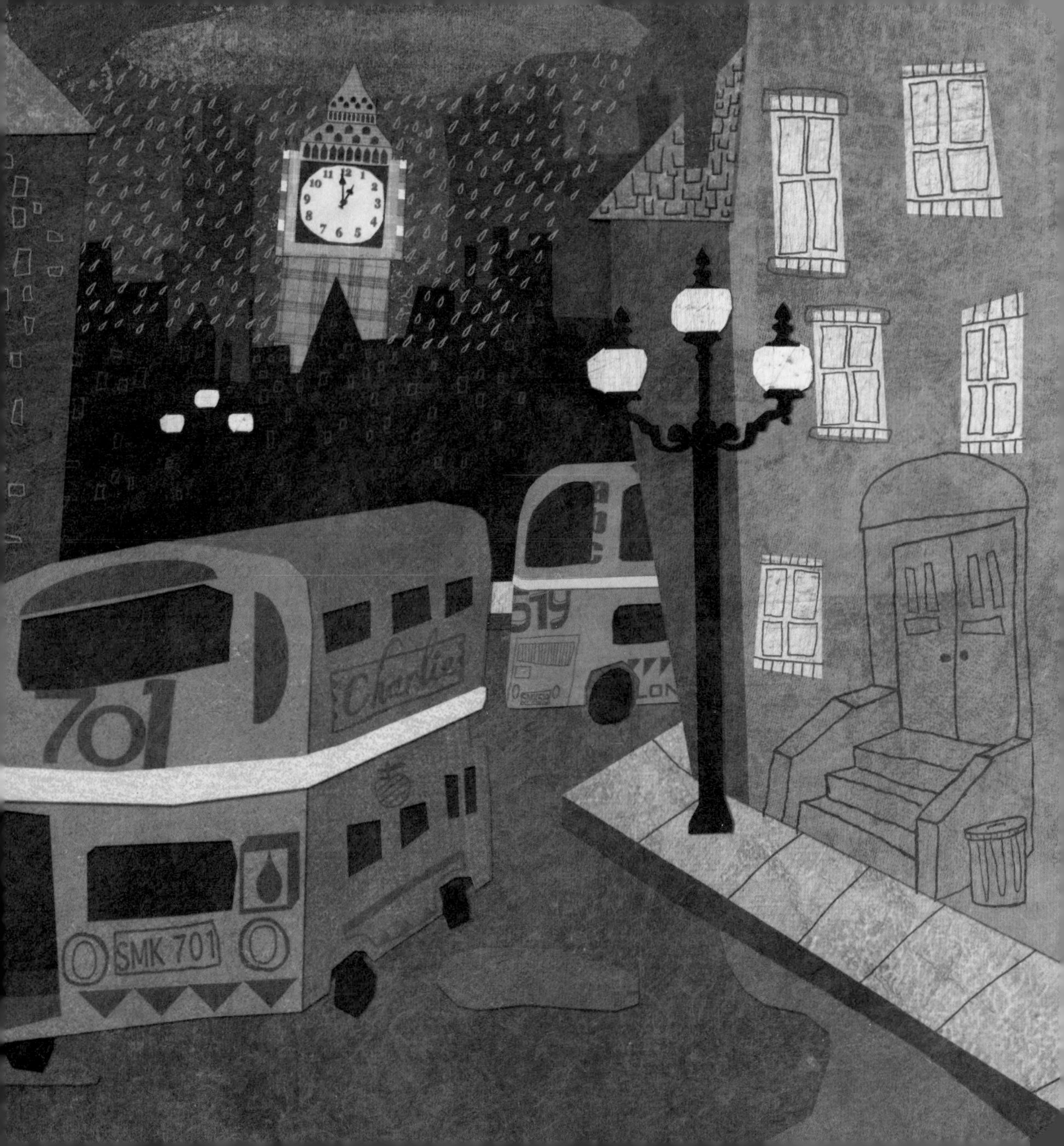
701
SMK 701
519

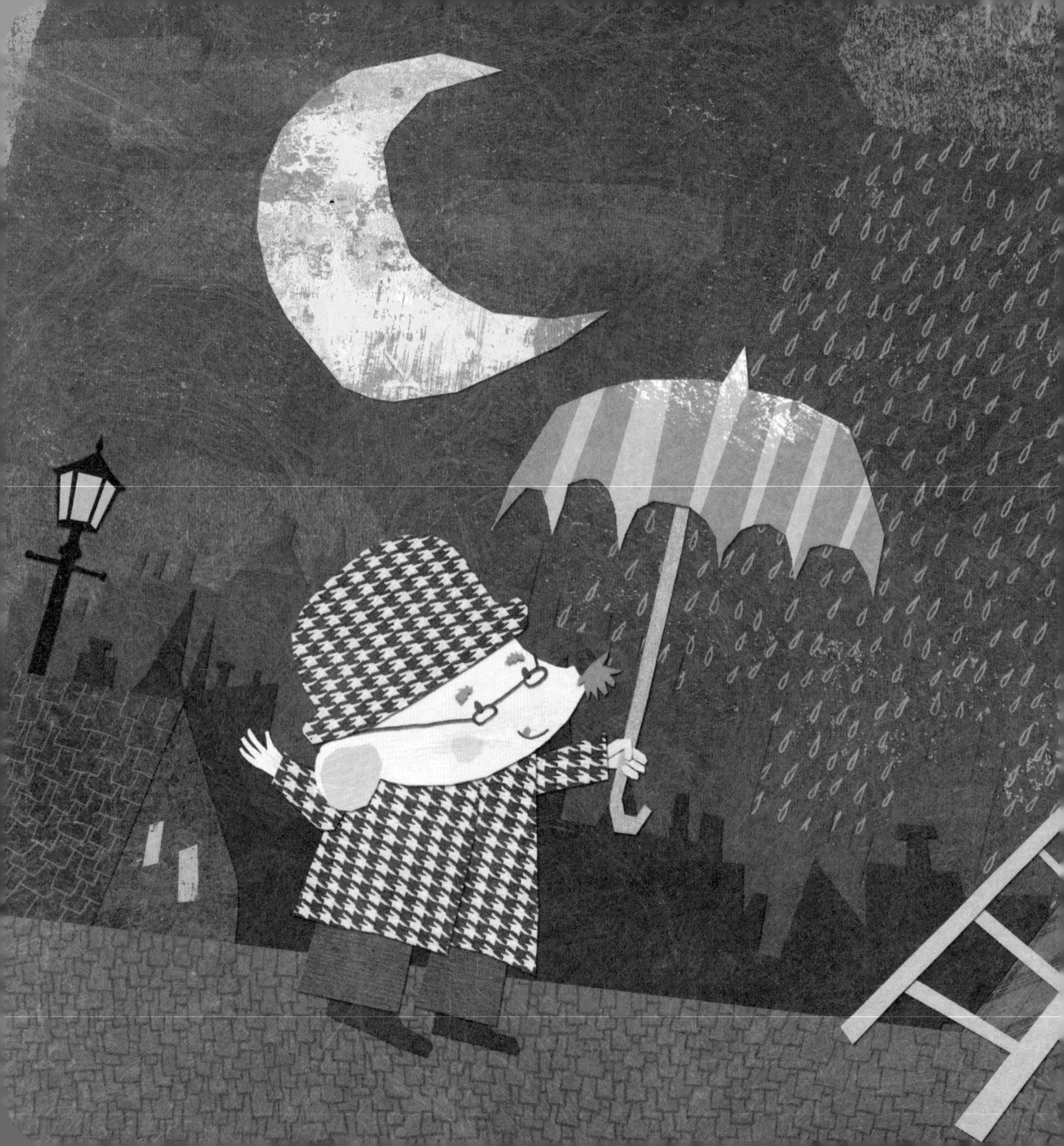

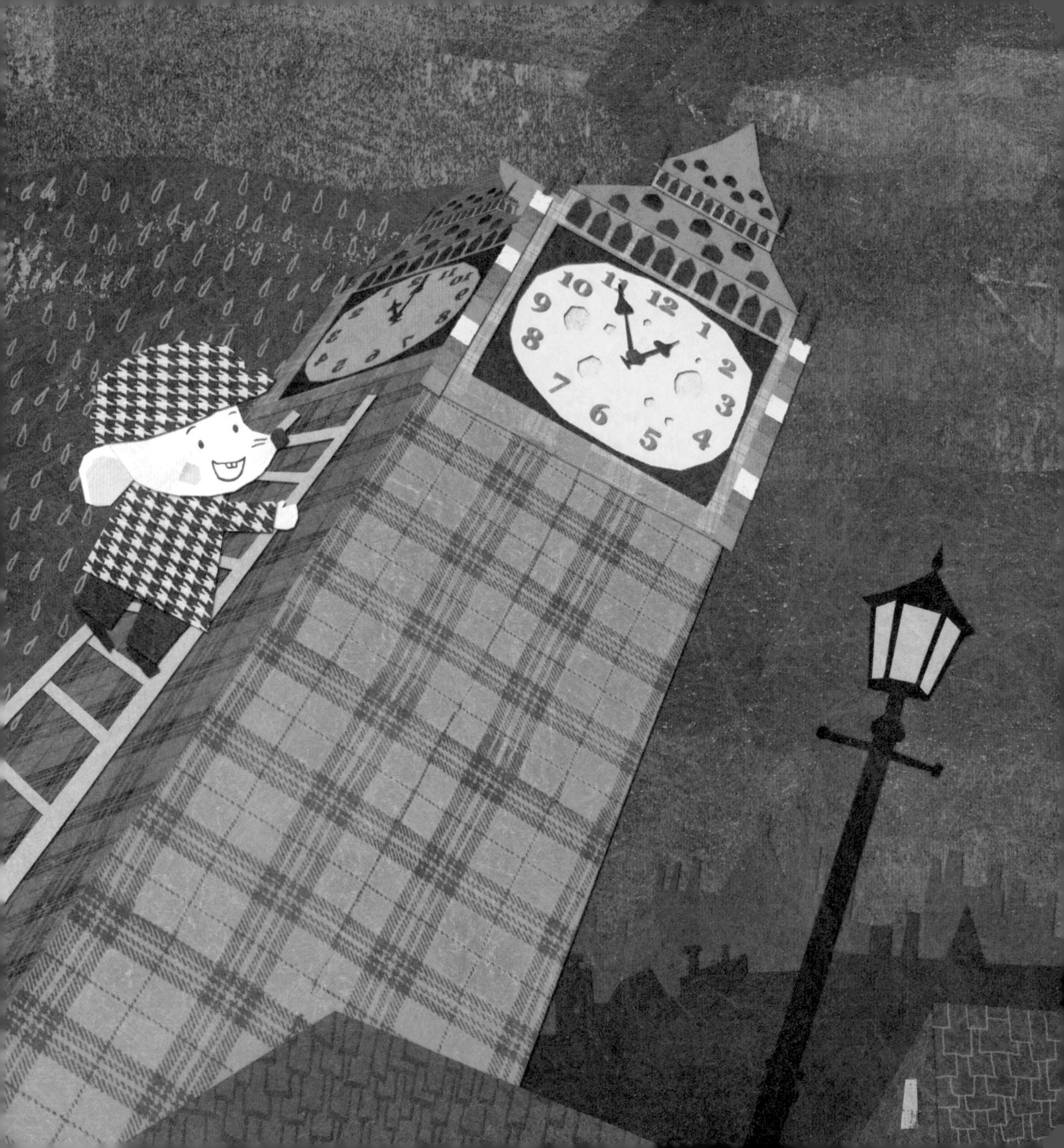

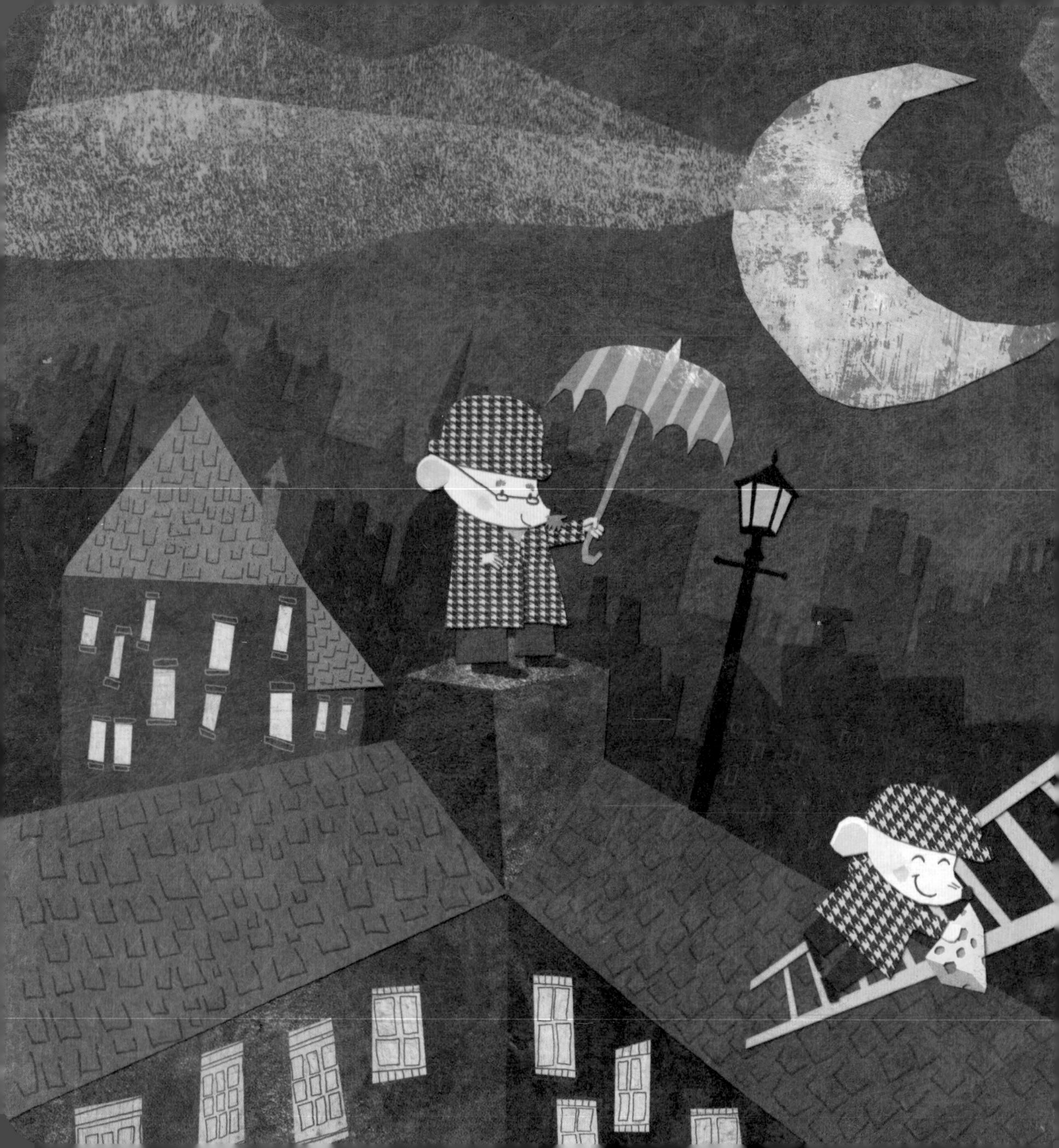